Boats! Boats! Boats!

Jo Cleland

Rourke
Publishing LLC
Vero Beach, Florida 32964

This book can be sung to the tune of "Row, Row, Row Your Boat."

www.rourkepublishing.com

PHOTO CREDITS: © Janice Richard, © Michael Walker, © Keith Binns: Cover; © Janice Richard: Title Page; © Kirill Zdorov: page 3; © Brian Raisbeck: page 4, 5; © Glenda Powers: page 6, 7; © Frank van Haalen: page 8, 9, 16, 17, 22, 23; © Matthew Ragen: page 10, 11, 23; Daniel MAR: page 12, 13; © Javier Fontanella: page 14, 15; © Ron Hohehaus: page 18, 19, 23; © Martin Kucera: page 20, 21; © Michael Walker: page 22;

Editor: Kelli Hicks

Cover and Interior designed by: Renee Brady

Library of Congress Cataloging-in-Publication Data

Cleland, Joann.
  Boats! boats! boats! / Jo Cleland.
     p. cm. -- (My first discovery library)
  Includes index.
  ISBN 978-1-60472-526-1
  1. Boats and boating --Juvenile literature.
  VM150 .C582 2009
  623.82 22
                              2008027361

Printed in the USA

CG/CG

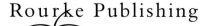

Rourke Publishing

www.rourkepublishing.com – rourke@rourkepublishing.com
Post Office Box 3328, Vero Beach, FL 32964

See the motorboat.

Watch the water spray.

See the sailboat glide along.

4

Watch it dip and sway.

5

See the rowboat go.

Watch it cross
the lake.

See the workers' fishing boat.

8

Watch the big
waves break.

9

See the lifeboat bob.

Watch it float away.

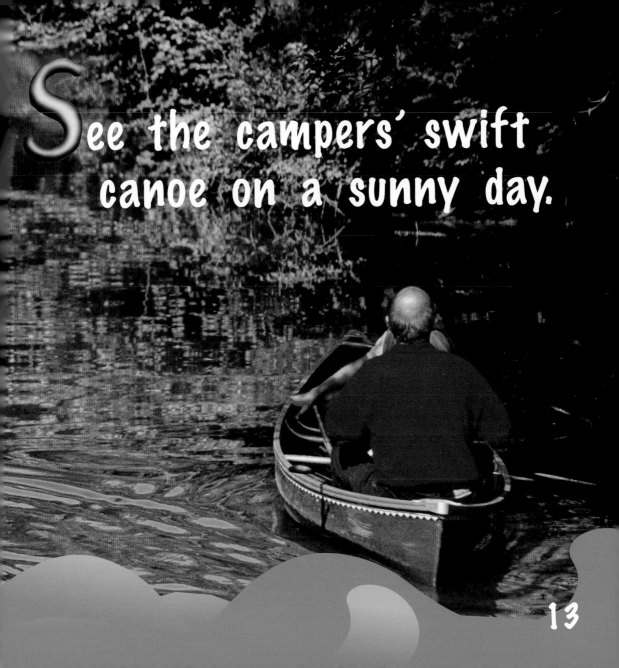

See the campers' swift canoe on a sunny day.

13

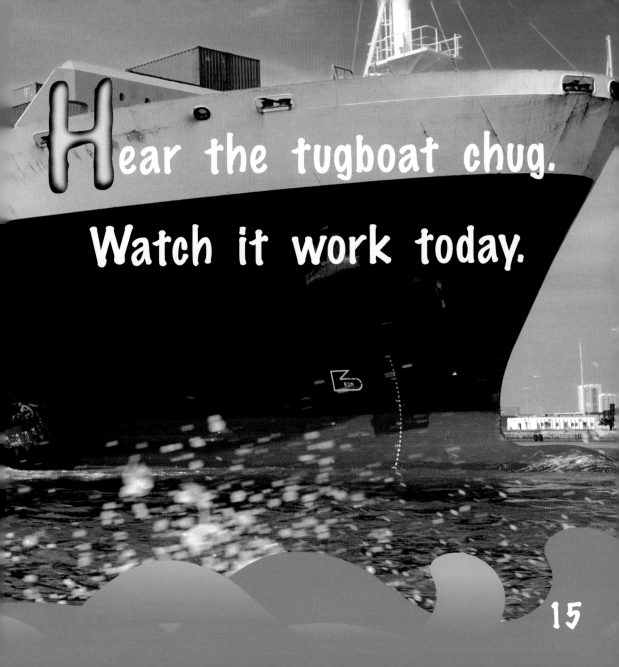

Hear the tugboat chug.

Watch it work today.

15

Hear the foghorn
honk and honk.

16

"Get out of my way!"

See my beach boat.

18

Hear me splash and play.

19

See the toy boat
 in my bath.

Lots of fun! Hooray!

21

Glossary

foghorn (FOG-horn): A foghorn is a horn for a boat. It is used on a foggy night to keep boats safe. The sound of a foghorn is a deep, low sound.

lake (LAKE): A lake is a big body of water with land around it. Most lakes are freshwater. They are bigger and deeper than ponds.

lifeboat (LIFE-boht): A small boat kept on a big ship for people to use in an emergency. Some lifeboats can carry 50 people.

beach (BEECH): The sandy land next to a body of water. Beaches can be found by oceans, rivers, or lakes.

waves (WAYVZ): The curls of water made by moving boats. Dolphins like to swim in boat waves.

Index

Further Reading

Armentrout, David and Patricia. *Ships*. Rourke, 2004.
Barton, Byron. *Boats*. Harper Collins, 1986.
Pallotta, Jerry. *The Boat Alphabet Book*. Charlesbridge, 1998.

Websites

http://pbskids.org/zoom/activities/sci/boatsafloat.html
http://www.gamerevolt.com/game/10946/Mini-Boat-Race.html
http://www.boatingsidekicks.com/besafe.htm

About the Author

Jo Cleland loves to write books, compose songs, and make games. She loves to read, sing, and play games with children.